AF605263

The Forever Kid

Elizabeth Mary Cummings
Illustrator Cheri Hughes

First published 2018

All inquiries should be made to the publishers.
Big Sky Publishing Pty Ltd
PO Box 303, Newport, NSW 2106, Australia
Phone: 1300 364 611   Fax: (61 2) 9918 2396
Email: info@bigskypublishing.com.au
Web: www.bigskypublishing.com.au

Cover Design and Typesetting: Cheri Hughes
Printed in China by Asia Pacific Offset Ltd
National Library of Australia Cataloguing-in-Publication entry (pbk and hbk)
Author: Elizabeth Mary Cummings
Title: The Forever Kid
ISBN: 978-1-925675-38-2 (paperback)
ISBN: 978-1-925675-39-9 (hardback)
Subjects: Family, Grief, Resilience.

For John-Aloysius and all Forever Kids – E.C.

For Mandi – C.H.

My family always celebrates birthdays.

The birthday person gets to choose their favourite food.

They choose their favourite games.

On my brother Johnny's birthday we always play cloud stories.

Today we are celebrating his birthday.

Here's the photo from Johnny's birthday last year.

Look! I am wearing his wombat t-shirt.

See Mum, Dad, my sister Pat, little Miley, and our dog, Barker.

All of us!

This is Johnny.

Johnny is not in that photo but we know he is with us.

Johnny our Forever Kid.

That's what we call him now.

Pat also likes Johnny's old wombat t-shirt.

It still smells a bit of Johnny.

Soft and fluffy, like clouds!

Miley giggles at the photo. 'My Johnny.'

Dad strokes her cheek. 'You have his dimples Miley!'

I look at the photo again. It's true – Johnny's dimples – in Miley's cheeks!

Johnny's favourite party food was cheesy-puffs.

In that photo Pat is laughing.

Cheesy-puffs everywhere!

Puffy yellow rings of cheesy-puffs on Pat's fingers!

Barker, on two hind legs, eating one.

Johnny taught him that trick!

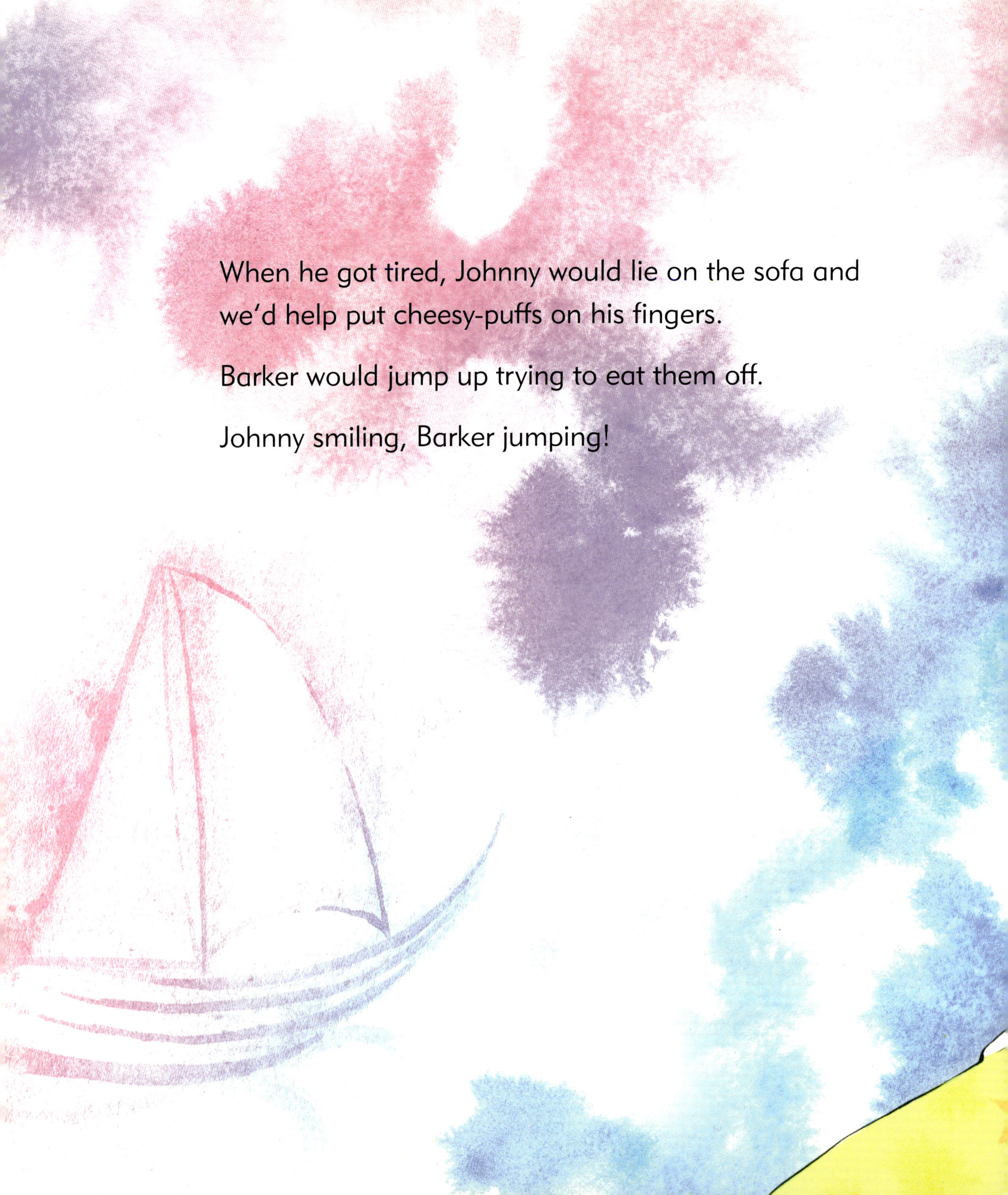

When he got tired, Johnny would lie on the sofa and we'd help put cheesy-puffs on his fingers.

Barker would jump up trying to eat them off.

Johnny smiling, Barker jumping!

Mum was never cross with Johnny even when he made Barker jump on the sofa.

Johnny got away with so much.

I used to think that wasn't fair.

Now I feel bad.

I wish Johnny could be here.

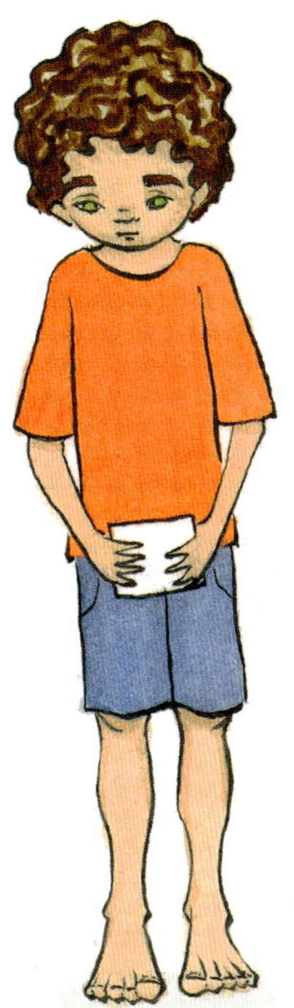

Everyone stops and remembers.

Johnny, our Forever Kid, who loved everything and everyone.

Especially cuddling little Miley.

Especially computer time with me.

Especially watching movies with Pat.

Especially building models with Dad.

Especially Mum's chocolate-chip cookies.

Most of all, telling cloud stories.

We used to spend ages lying in the backyard making up stories about the clouds with Johnny.

Johnny loved those cloud stories.

Even when he could no longer do all the other things he loved. He always loved the cloud stories.

Always.

So do I.

Even now.

It feels like Johnny is with me.

My big brother.

My never-growing-up brother.

My Forever-Kid brother, Johnny.

Miley gets down from Dad's knee.

'I want Johnny cloud stories!'

Dad stands up. 'Yes, let's do it!'

He follows Miley outside into the garden.

Mum lets Barker put his paw on the sofa next to her.

Pat puts the photo back on the special birthday table.

Pat and I look at each other.

'You too Mum!'